For Melly—M.M.

This first edition published in the United States in 2003 by MONDO Publishing,
by arrangement with Macmillan Children's Books.

Text copyright © 2003 by Miriam Moss
Illustrations copyright © 2003 by Jutta Bücker

Printed in Belgium by Proost

For information contact:
MONDO Publishing
980 Avenue of the Americas
New York, NY 10018
Visit our web site at http://www.mondopub.com

03 04 05 06 07 08 09 10   HC 9 8 7 6 5 4 3 2 1
ISBN 1-59336-060-6 (hardcover)   ISBN 1-59336-061-4 (pbk.)

Library of Congress Cataloging-in-Publication Data

Moss, Miriam.
Wiley and Jasper / Miriam Moss ; illustrated by Jutta Bücker.
        p. cm.
Summary: Wiley the boy and Jasper the dog are afraid of each other, until the day a
thunderstorm leads them to seek the same shelter.
ISBN 1-59336-060-6 — ISBN 1-59336-061-4 (pbk.)
[1. Fear—Fiction. 2. Dogs—Fiction. 3. Thunderstorms—Fiction.] I. Bücker, Jutta, ill.II.
Title.

    PZ7.M85353Wg 2003
    [E]-dc21

2003050967

Miriam Moss

Wiley and Jasper

Illustrated by Jutta Bücker

Along a quiet street high up on a hill, two houses stand side by side.

Wiley lives with his mom and dad in one house. Jasper lives with Grandpa in the other.

Jasper is a dog who pretends to be big and brave. He barks loudly and guards the gate.

But really he's scared of falling leaves, thunderstorms, and even cats!

Most of all, Jasper is scared of kids. When Wiley visits Grandpa, Jasper hides in the bedroom.

Wiley is a little boy who also pretends to be big and brave. He climbs trees and swings higher than anyone else.

But really he's scared of monsters, getting lost, and the dark.

Most of all, Wiley is scared of dogs. When Grandpa visits Wiley, Jasper stays at home.

On Grandpa's birthday,
Dad packed up a picnic basket
and everyone climbed into the car.

Wiley looked out of one window.
Jasper looked out of the other.

On the top of a hill, Mom parked the car.
"Here we are!" she said.
Wiley and Jasper jumped out, raced around
the car—and bumped right into one another.
They took one look at each other and ran off
in opposite directions.

Mom and Dad set out the picnic
while Jasper and Wiley explored.

"Come and get it!" shouted Dad, just as
a gust of wind blew the napkins away.

"Wi-leeey!" called Mom, as the sky grew dark.
"Jaaaas-per!" called Grandpa, as the first drops of
rain plopped onto the blanket.
But the wind blew their voices away.
And the rain poured down.

Wiley was down at the bottom of the hill
watching puddles grow.

CRACK!

A flash of lightning lit up the sky.

Wiley raced to a
small barn nearby.

The door creaked
shut behind him.

Wiley stood in the dark, his heart thumping.
He reached out and felt his way along a wall.

Something moved. Wiley froze.
A dark head and two eyes appeared.

BOOM!

Thunder crashed outside. Wiley jumped.
The thing near him whimpered, and then the
whole barn was lit by a great flash of lightning.
Jasper stared at Wiley. Wiley stared at Jasper.

Jasper was trembling, so Wiley spoke
into the darkness, "I'm scared, too."
And slowly he stretched out his hand
toward Jasper.

At first Jasper backed away,
but then he crept closer and gently
licked Wiley's hand.
Very slowly, Jasper moved closer,
and then closer, to Wiley.

Outside the storm raged,
while Wiley stroked Jasper's soft
fur. Soon Jasper's head was
resting in Wiley's lap. Wiley
sighed and fell asleep, breathing
in the warm dog smell.

And when the storm was over,
that's how Grandpa found them,
all curled up and fast asleep in the straw.

Now, when Wiley visits Jasper—
it's playtime!

And when Jasper visits Wiley, Wiley lifts
Jasper's furry ear and reminds him that he's
the best dog in the whole, wide world.